This book is dedicated to all of the wonderful people who have helped me to find and use my own "NO".
I love you all so very much.

It's my hope that "The Little Girl Who Lost Her 'NO'" will give children the wisdom, understanding and courage to find and use their own 'NO' as it is needed throughout their lives.

"A no uttered from the deepest conviction is better than a 'yes' merely uttered to please, or worse, to avoid trouble."- Mahatma Gandhi

Once there was a girl, about your age, who was missing her "NO"!

She was always saying "yes" to everyone and everything.

But when she wanted to say "no", her "NO" was nowhere to be found!

The little girl always said "yes" to her parents because she knew that listening to them was the right thing to do.

OUR FAMILY

She enjoyed making them proud and loved them both very much! And they loved her very, very much, too!

When her mom asked her to make her bed or clean up her room, she always said, "yes".

When her dad asked her to do her homework or play with her baby brother, she always said, "yes".

Sometimes at school, her teacher, Mrs. Miller, would ask her to collect everyone's worksheets.

The little girl always said "yes" to Mrs. Miller because she liked being a good helper. It made her feel good about herself to have an important job at school.

She didn't mind saying "yes" to her parents or her teacher, but sometimes the little girl wanted to tell people "no", especially when they asked her to do things she really didn't want to do.

There was just one problem... she couldn't find her "NO"!

She looked for it EVERYWHERE!

Where did her "NO" go?

First, she looked under her bed.

Nope....no "NO" under there!

Did I leave my "NO" under the bed???

Then she looked inside of her toy box,
but her "NO" was not in there.

Hmmm.....maybe
I left my "NO" in
the toy box....

She even looked in the cookie jar!!!

But her "NO" wasn't in there either...

just some chocolate chip cookies.

She needed to find her "NO" soon because there were times when she REALLY didn't want to say 'yes' at all!

Like the day at school when Jimmy Stevens, the school bully, came up to her at lunch and yelled "Give me your cookies!"

The little girl didn't say "no" because she was afraid.

Instead she just said 'Ok, yes, here you go", and handed her cookies over to Jimmy.

Saying "yes" to Jimmy didn't feel good at all, but when he yelled at her, she couldn't find her "NO"!

She said "yes" instead of saying "no", and now she felt MAD!

A week later, she was sitting at her desk taking a spelling test.

She studied very hard every night for the test and was sure she would ace it!

Emily Connelly sat next to her in class.

After Mrs. Miller handed out the spelling tests and walked back to her desk, Emily whispered to the little girl, "Hey! How do you spell 'action'? I don't wanna fail the test! C'mon, tell me!"

The little girl wanted to say "no". She worked hard studying the spelling words all week.

It wasn't fair that Emily would pass the test by cheating.

She wanted to say 'No, Emily, I'm not giving you the answers", but just like with Jimmy and the cookies, she couldn't find her "NO"!

All that would come out of her mouth was, "Yes, Emily. Action. A-c-t-i-o-n."

SHHHH!

"No talking!" shouted Mrs. Miller.

Whew! The little girl could have gotten into BIG trouble if Mrs. Miller would have caught her giving Emily answers to the spelling test!

She didn't feel good about cheating, but when Emily asked her for the answers, she couldn't find her "NO".

She said "yes" instead and now she felt GUILTY.

On Thursday, the little girl invited her neighbor friend, Glenda, over to her house.

While they were playing, Glenda noticed the little girl's stuffed animal, Scruffy.

Scruffy was a cute black and white puppy and he was the little girl's absolute favorite of all of the stuffed animals in her entire collection!

The little girl remembered what had happened all of the other times she had let Glenda borrow her stuff.

Glenda borrowed her doll, but never gave it back!

She borrowed a book, but had ripped several of the pages!

And then there was the time Glenda borrowed her markers. When she returned them, the purple one was missing!

The little girl really liked her friend, Glenda, and wanted to make her happy, but Scruffy was her favorite stuffed animal of all. She didn't want anything bad happening to him!

She tried to say "no" to Glenda, but all that would come out was "Yes, ok, you can borrow Scruffy."

Again, she couldn't find her "NO"!

As much as she wanted to say it, it wouldn't come out!

She said "yes" to Glenda instead and now she felt SAD.

That weekend she was sitting at the table eating dinner with her family.

Her mom asked, 'Why aren't you eating your peas?"

"I don't like peas, Mommy," she replied.

"But sweetie, you always eat peas. Since when do you not like peas? Now eat them before they get cold."

"NO." the little girl said firmly.

"What did you say?" asked her mother.

"I.........said................................

"NOOOOOOOOOOOOOOO!" she screamed, at the top of her lungs!

"NO!!! I don't like peas!"

"And NO you can't have my cookies, Jimmy!"

"And NO, I'm not giving you the answers, Emily!"

"And NO you can't borrow Scruffy, Glenda!"

"NO! NO! NO! I definitely do NOT like peas!"

The little girl shouted so loudly that her baby brother began to cry!

She was shocked! All this time her "NO" had been missing and FINALLY she found it!

It was hiding inside of her all along!

"I'm so sorry for yelling at you, Mommy," she cried.

"I didn't mean to. It's just that I couldn't find my "NO" and then, all of the sudden, it finally came out!

"It's okay, honey," her mom said. "I'm glad you told me how you REALLY feel. Next time, I'll be sure to listen to what you're trying to tell me, but I want you to tell me your feelings without shouting. And I don't want you to eat peas if you really don't like them."

26

That's when the little girl realized that it was okay to tell others how she REALLY felt and to even say "no" to them if she needed to.

I found it! I found my "NO"!

She FINALLY found her "NO" and it was okay to use it!

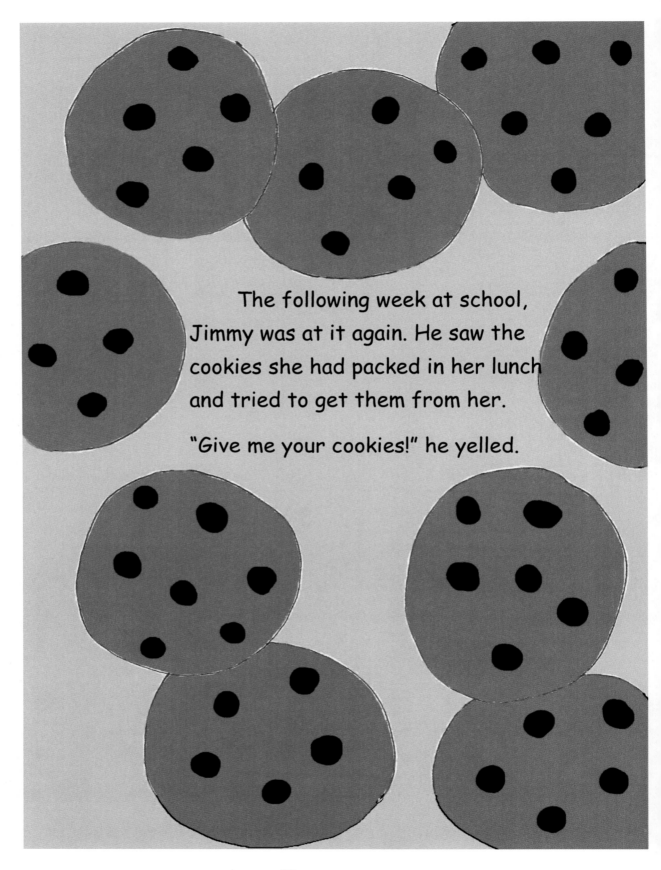

The following week at school, Jimmy was at it again. He saw the cookies she had packed in her lunch and tried to get them from her.

"Give me your cookies!" he yelled.

Only THIS time, the little girl was NOT afraid to tell him "no"! She quickly jumped up from her seat and shouted, "NO! These are MY cookies, Jimmy! Get your own!"

Jimmy was stunned...no one had ever stood up to him before!

He just turned and walked away.

The little girl had found her "NO" and now she felt
BRAVE!

Later that day, it was time for another weekly spelling test.

Once again, Emily leaned over and whispered to the little girl, "Hey, how do you spell 'direction'? Are you gonna tell me or not?"

The little girl quickly replied, "No…N-O. That's how I spell it" and raised her hand to let Mrs. Miller know that Emily was trying to cheat on the test.

"Emily, you know cheating is wrong. I will have to call your parents about this."

"I'm glad you told me," Mrs. Miller said to the little girl. "You did the right thing."

She had used her "NO" with Emily and now she felt
PROUD!

That evening, while she was playing at Glenda's house, she told Glenda that she wanted Scruffy back now.

"But...but...but...can't I just keep him one more week??? Pleeeeasssssseeeeee," Glenda begged.

The little girl really cared about her friend Glenda but she also really loved Scruffy and she wanted him back now.

She didn't want to hurt Glenda's feelings, but she didn't want to miss or worry about Scruffy anymore either.

"No, I'm sorry, Glenda. I'm going to need Scruffy back now," she said firmly.

"Okay. Here you go," Glenda said as she handed Scruffy back to the little girl and smiled.

The little girl had used her "NO" to get Scruffy back,
and now she felt HAPPY!

A few nights later, her family had peas again at dinner.

"Honey, would you like some peas," her mom asked.

"No. No thank you, Mommy. I don't want any," she replied.

Her mom smiled at her. "Okay, I'm glad you told me. And good job using your "NO" calmly this time", she said. "I'm very proud of you!"

She still listened to her parents and teacher, and said "yes" whenever they told her to do something important or asked her to help them.

But she remembered to use her "NO" anytime she needed to with her friends, classmates, bullies, or for anyone or anything that made her feel bad or upset inside.

The little girl had finally found her missing "NO" and she never wanted to lose it again!

Let's practice saying 'NO' with her on the count of three....Ready?

One.....two....three...

NOOOOOOOOOO OOOOOOOOOOOO OOOOOOO!!!

VERY GOOD!!!

The End ☺

Discussion Questions

1. Was there ever a time when you said 'yes' to someone, but you really wanted to say 'no'? If so, what was it and how did you feel about it?

2. When have you said 'no' to something or someone and felt brave, happy or proud?

3. Which character do you think was the hardest for the little girl to say 'no' to at first...her best friend, Glenda or the school bully, Jimmy? Why?

About the Author

Amy M. Starkey, affectionately known as 'Miss Amy' by all of her students, has worked with children of all ages and ability levels for over 14 years as both a pediatric occupational therapy assistant and a children's yoga instructor.

She's the owner of "Yoga-2-Go, LLC", a children's yoga business which allows her to combine her passion for teaching yoga with her love for helping children grow, heal, discover, connect, imagine, and believe in themselves!

"The Little Girl Who Lost Her 'NO!'" was inspired by one of her weekly kids' yoga classes. Using yoga poses, games and stories, the class taught the students how to be more confident and assertive, to identify their emotions, and to use their voices to express themselves and their inner experience.

She lives in Canton, Ohio with her beloved pup, Dozer (who just so happens to bear a very close resemblance to 'Scruffy').

After finding her own missing 'NO', she now freely uses it as often as necessary. ☺

Check out her website at: www.missamysyoga2go.com

Made in the USA
Columbia, SC
01 October 2020